Sheep Take a Hike

Nancy Shaw

Sheep Take a Hike

Illustrated by Margot Apple

Houghton Mifflin Company   Boston

Also by Nancy Shaw and illustrated by Margot Apple:

Sheep in a Jeep

Sheep on a Ship

Sheep in a Shop

Sheep Out to Eat

Library of Congress Cataloging-in-Publication Data

Shaw, Nancy (Nancy E.)
  Sheep take a hike / Nancy Shaw ; illustrated by Margot
Apple.
   p.   cm.
  Summary: Having gotten lost on a chaotic hike in the great
outdoors, the sheep find their way back by following the trail of
wool they have left.
    RNF ISBN 0-395-68394-7   PAP ISBN 0-395-81658-0
    [1. Sheep — Fiction. 2. Hiking — Fiction. 3. Stories in rhyme.]
I. Apple, Margot, ill. II. Title.
PZ8.3.S5334Sk   1994   93-30725
[E] — dc20   CIP
                            AC

Printed in China

SCP 28 27 26 25 24 23 22 21

4500501761

To Nancy Weiss
—N.S.

To Allison, Daniel, Nancy,
Scott and Fred
—M.A.

Morning's here! It's warm and clear!

Sheep load up their hiking gear.

Compass, whistles, drinks, and snacks
Go in packs upon their backs.

They trot along a hiking trail

Up the hill and down the dale.

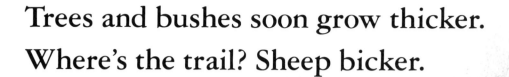

Trees and bushes soon grow thicker.
Where's the trail? Sheep bicker.

Sheep squeeze through the trees.
Sheep rush through underbrush.

Thorns dig. Prickers snag.
Sheep zig. Sheep zag.

Fog comes up. The ground feels damp.

On and on, sheep tramp.

Sheep stomp into a swamp.
Moosh! Goosh! Boggy tracks!

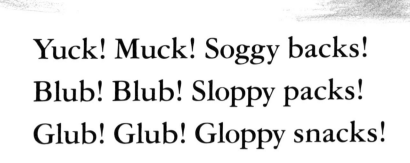

Yuck! Muck! Soggy backs!
Blub! Blub! Sloppy packs!
Glub! Glub! Gloppy snacks!

The compass sinks. They're in dismay.
How can they ever find their way?

Sheep climb out of the slime.

They look around, and soon they find

Woolly fuzz they left behind.

Sheep won't stray—
They've marked the way!

Now they're on the hiking path.

What more could they want? . . . A bath!

Sheep trot homeward. Rain pours.

What a day for the great outdoors!